THE DOODLES OF SAM DIBBLE

Double Trouble

THE DOODLES

OF SAM DIBBLE

Double Trouble

by J. Press
illustrated by Michael Kline

Grosset & Dunlap
An Imprint of Penguin Group (USA) Inc.

GROSSET & DUNLAP
Published by the Penguin Group
Penguin Group (USA) Inc., 375 Hudson Street, New York, New York 10014, USA
Penguin Group (Canada), 90 Eglinton Avenue East, Suite 700, Toronto,
Ontario M4P 2Y3, Canada (a division of Pearson Penguin Canada Inc.)
Penguin Books Ltd, 80 Strand, London WC2R 0RL, England
Penguin Ireland, 25 St Stephen's Green, Dublin 2, Ireland (a division of Penguin Books Ltd)
Penguin Group (Australia), 707 Collins Street, Melbourne, Victoria 3008, Australia
(a division of Pearson Australia Group Pty Ltd)
Penguin Books India Pvt Ltd, 11 Community Centre, Panchsheel Park,
New Delhi—110 017, India
Penguin Group (NZ), 67 Apollo Drive, Rosedale, Auckland 0632, New Zealand
(a division of Pearson New Zealand Ltd)
Penguin Books, Rosebank Office Park, 181 Jan Smuts Avenue,
Parktown North 2193, South Africa
Penguin China, B7 Jaiming Center, 27 East Third Ring Road North,
Chaoyang District, Beijing 100020, China

Penguin Books Ltd, Registered Offices: 80 Strand, London WC2R 0RL, England

Text copyright © 2013 by Judy Press. Illustrations copyright © 2013 by
Michael Kline. All rights reserved. Published by Grosset & Dunlap, a division of
Penguin Young Readers Group, 345 Hudson Street, New York, New York 10014.
GROSSET & DUNLAP is a trademark of Penguin Group (USA) Inc. Printed in the U.S.A.

Library of Congress Cataloging-in-Publication Data is available.

ISBN 978-0-448-46108-3   10 9 8 7 6 5 4 3 2 1

For the boys: Nat, Noah, Mahlon, and Isaac—JP

And for my offspring Steve and Jon . . . U guys rock!—MK

Chapter One
Rocket-Powered Sneaker Doodle

I, Samuel P. Dibble, can curl my tongue, wiggle my ears, and win burping contests. But what I like to do best is doodle.

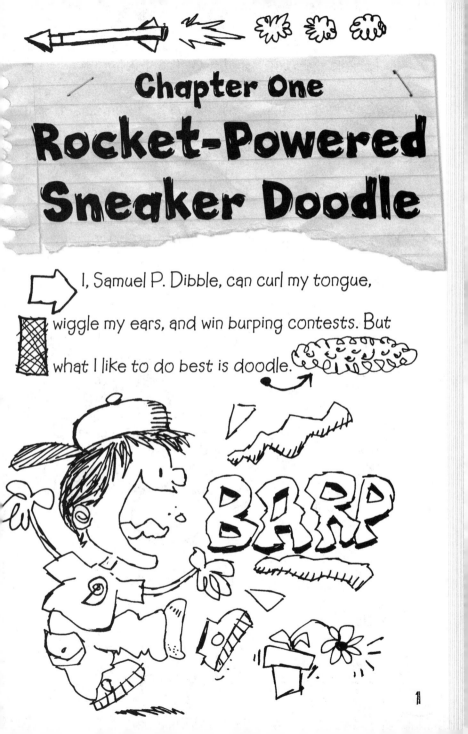

BARP

I think doodling is a lot of fun. It's like taking your pen for a walk and going someplace you've never been before.

My grandpa Dibble says all Dibbles doodle. "Why, even Great-Great-Great-Grandpa Mickey Angelo doodled."

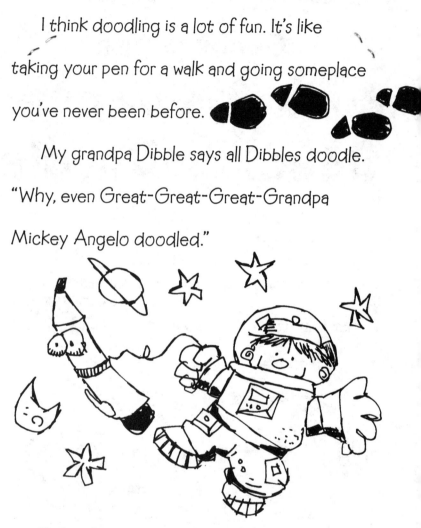

"What happened to him?" I asked Grandpa.

"He got in trouble, yes indeed. Doodled

on the ceiling of a church," Grandpa told me.

I go to Colfax Elementary

School, and my teacher's

name is Mrs. Hennessey.

She has radar implanted

in her head that beeps when

kids are fooling around.

In school, we were learning about our government and how presidents get elected. Mrs. H. told us that the next Tuesday was Election Day, when people vote for president.

Here's why I never want to be president of the United States:

1. Presidents can't pick their noses because the whole world will see them doing it.

2. A president doesn't get an allowance, so he can't buy video games.

3. If a president goes trick-or-treating, everyone will think he's wearing a president costume.

A+ Mrs. H. was busy working at her desk. We were supposed to be reading a book about the presidents, but I was doodling in my notebook.

It was a doodle of sneakers that have rocket-propelled engines on the back.

Even the president of the United States would want a pair, so he wouldn't have to use *Air Force One* to fly places.

Suddenly, Max Baxter jumped up out of his seat. "Mrs. Hennessey, Sam's doodling! I saw him do it."

Max is the biggest tattletale in third grade. Everyone calls him "Wax" because one time we had a contest to see who could pick the most wax out of our ears, and he won.

And here's the thing that stinks worse than my gym socks: Wax's dad is my mom's boyfriend!

Mrs. H. told Wax to sit down and me to pay attention. Then she said, "Class, every four years our country votes for president. Who can tell me what our president does?"

Nicole McDonald raised her hand. "The president tells countries to be friends so they don't go to war," she said.

Then Meghan Diaz said, "The president helps protect the environment so we don't have pollution."

Meghan and Nicole sit next to each other in the back of the room. They dress alike and tell everyone they're twins, but they're really just best friends. Girls do silly things like that.

"Those are both good," Mrs. H. responded. "Anyone else?"

"The president's not allowed to lie," Cookie added. "Abraham Lincoln was called 'Honest Abe' because he always told the truth."

Cookie's real name is Reginald Cook, and he's my second-best friend.

No one gets too close to Cookie because he farts.

Then Wax raised his hand. "The president's not allowed to swear," he said. "It says so in the Constitution."

NO SWEARING

Duh, everyone knows that presidents swear. My grandpa Dibble said he heard George Washington say a bad word when his mom took away his superhero action figures.

"Okay, class, now I want you to write a letter to our president," Mrs. H. said. "Tell him about yourself and what you would do if you were president."

Here's my letter:

Dear Mr. President,

My name is Sam Dibble. If I were president

of the United States, I'd give money to poor

people so they could buy food and toys for their

kids. Do you like to doodle? I do, but sometimes

it gets me into trouble. Do you have a basketball

hoop in your backyard? Are you really tall?

Thank you.

Your friend,

Samuel P. Dibble

I turned my letter over and doodled on the back.

One day I'm going to meet the president, and we'll be best friends!

Chapter Two
A Gross Pizza Doodle

After Mrs. H. collected our letters, she told us some exciting news! We were going to elect a class president!

"Today is Tuesday," she said. "On Friday we'll vote. The class president should be someone who sets an example of good behavior and is helpful to others. He or she also should be someone who you think will be a responsible leader."

Everyone started talking about how cool it would be to be class president.

"Settle down," Mrs. H. said. "Being class president is a serious job. The class president will help me make some of the class rules. Also, the president will help me pick some of the other students for jobs, like messenger or pet monitor or cleanup monitor," she continued.

Rachel Woolsey raised her hand. "Mrs. Hennessey, I'd like to run for president."

Rachel's the most popular girl in my class, and she hates me. One time at lunch I slurped spaghetti through my teeth, and she said I was the grossest kid in third grade.

"Thank you, Rachel," Mrs. H. said.

My best friend, Robert Chen, sits next

POPULAR

to me. He's really smart and lets me copy off him.

"Sam, if Rachel is president, she'll make a rule that the boys have to do girly things," he whispered.

Yuck! I don't want to do that!

Next, Wax raised his hand. "I want to be president," he declared. "And when I get elected, we'll have pizza for lunch every day."

Then Wax shot a look at me. "And I know just who I'll make cleanup monitor!"

"We need one other candidate," Mrs. H.

continued, looking around the room.

I looked over at Wax. He was making a list

in his notebook. It was probably a list of all the

horrible things he'd make me do.

Maybe I should run.

Here's why I wanted to be class president:

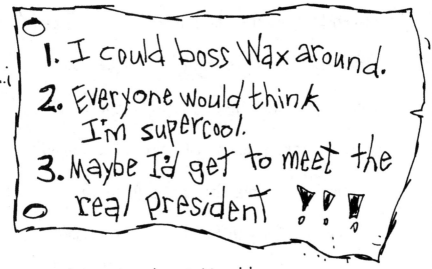

1. I could boss Wax around.
2. Everyone would think I'm supercool.
3. Maybe I'd get to meet the real president !!!

I raised my hand. Mrs. H. wrote my name

on the whiteboard next to Rachel's and Wax's

names.

"Now, class, you can get up out of your seats and talk to the candidates."

Robert leaned over to me. "I can be your campaign manager," he offered. "I helped my mom get elected captain of her bowling team."

"That's awesome. You're hired!" I said.

"I'm voting for you, Sam!" Cookie shouted as he ran up to me. "You'll make a great president."

Then Wax came over. "When I'm president, I'm outlawing doodling!" he threatened.

Figures Wax would do something like that. It's like the time at lunch when he snuck something into my apple.

Wax walked away, and Mrs. H. said, "Everyone, please return to your seats and gather up your things. The last bell's about to ring."

When I got home, I told Grandpa Dibble that I was running for class president.

"One time I ran for class president,"

Grandpa said.

"What happened, Grandpa? Did you win?"

"Nah, some kid ran faster than me, and he

won!"

I knew I'd need a lot more than a fast pair

of legs to win this race!

Chapter Three
A Fighting-Fish Doodle

The next morning in school, Mrs. H. said

we were going to play Meet the Candidates.

I didn't get it. Everyone already knew who

we were, so why did they have to meet us?

"Here's how it works," she explained. "You'll ask the candidate a question, and they'll have one minute to give you their answer."

"Mrs. Hennessey, can we practice before we start?" Rachel asked.

"That's a good idea, Rachel. Use the next few minutes to think of answers to questions your classmates might ask you."

Robert and I decided to practice over in the Science Corner. That's where we kept our class pets.

Fernando is a betta fish. He has to be all by himself in the aquarium because he fights with other fish.

Fluffernutter is a golden hamster. She has peanut butter-colored fur. Her cage is on the table next to Fernando.

There are other cool things in the Science Corner, too. Cookie brought in a horseshoe crab shell he found on the beach. Mrs. H. said he could put it out on the table.

Wax once brought in a dinosaur bone. He said it was from a real dinosaur, but Mrs. H.

found out it was just a turkey bone and made

him take it home.

GOBBLE GOBBLE!

Robert and I pulled our chairs close

together so we could talk about what I was

supposed to do. BLAH BLAH BLAH

"What if I don't know the answer to

a question?" I asked Robert. "Can I make

something up?"

"That's what all politicians do," Robert said. "So let's practice. I'll ask you a question, and you give me the answer."

"Ask me something easy," I said. "Like, 'What's your name?' Or 'How old are you?'"

"That's too easy!" Robert said. "How about this: If you were elected class president, what would you change?"

"I know the answer! We wouldn't get homework on my birthday."

SAM DIBBLE DAY

NO HOMEWORK!

"Not bad," Robert said as we walked back to our desks. "I think you're ready."

Mrs. H. asked the candidates to stand together in the front of the room.

"Raise your hand and wait until I call on you before asking your question," she told the class.

Meghan raised her hand first. "This is for Sam," she said. "If you were president, how would you change the school lunch?"

"We'd have pizza for lunch every day!" I answered.

T-BONE, Ice cReam, and French FRy PiZZA!

Wax jumped up and down. "That's not fair! Sam copied off me."

copier

"Settle down, Max," Mrs. H. said. "Sam just agrees with your idea."

Next, Cookie raised his hand. "This question is for Wax. Why should we vote for you?"

Ticket

"Because I'm giving everyone tickets to a Little League baseball game," Wax answered.

PEANUTS

"The games are free, Wax!" I shouted. "No one needs a ticket."

"Sam, raise your hand if you have something to say," Mrs. H. warned.

Then Nicole's hand shot up. "This question is for Rachel. If you're president, what will you do?"

"I'll have us partner with the kindergarten kids and help them read," Rachel said with a smile.

Everyone clapped except for me. What if I got partnered with Lucy? She's in kindergarten, and she's Wax's annoying little sister.

"Thank you, candidates," Mrs. H. said.

"It's going to be a tough decision. Any one of you would make a good president. On Friday, before we vote, you'll each have a chance to give a short campaign speech. Be sure to choose your words wisely!"

Chapter Four
A Lincoln Penny Doodle

After lunch, Mrs. H. handed out assignment sheets with questions about the presidents. "Pick a past president of the United States," she said. "Then use your time in the library to do research and fill in the answers."

The library in my school has books, magazines, a media center, and computers. We're allowed to take a book home, but if we forget to return it, we get into big trouble.

Mrs. Booker is the school librarian. She
was waiting for us when we got to the library.

@ "Class, please take your seats," she
said. "Today you'll use the Internet and our
collection of biographies to work on your
assignment."

Robert, Cookie, and I each took a seat in
front of one of the computers. Then Wax sat
down at the computer next to us.

COMPUTER WORM!

On the wall above us was a poster that said

Books: Food for the Brain.

"Dribble, you're going to lose the election," Wax announced. "No one's going to vote for a kid who doodles."

"Today's Wednesday, and voting's on Friday," Robert said. "And anything can happen."

"Which president are you picking?" Cookie

asked me.

"I'm picking Abraham Lincoln," I answered.

"He has his picture on a penny, and he had

a dog, two goats, and a turkey in the White

House."

"Grover Cleveland has his picture on a

thousand-dollar bill," Cookie said. "I think I'll

pick him."

"I picked William Henry Harrison," Wax bragged. "He was president for only one month, so I won't have to answer any of the questions."

WRITE QUESTIONS IN THIS BOX ➝ □

Wax went off to look for a book while I typed in "Abraham Lincoln" on the computer.

I looked over the site. "Hey, Robert, it says here that Lincoln was born in a log cabin."

"Yeah, and he wrote the Gettysburg Address," Robert said. "It's a really famous speech."

A. LINCOLN
WHITE house
1863 N. Gettysburg
Pennsylvania

That reminded me that Mrs. H. said the

candidates have to give a speech before we

can vote.

Maybe I can give the

Gettysburg Address. No

one will even remember that

Lincoln did it first.

Cookie leaned over and whispered in my

ear, "Wax is telling everyone to boo when you

give your speech."

"Mine will be so good they'll all cheer," I

reassured Cookie.

When we finished our assignment, Mrs.

Booker said, "If anyone has a reference book,

35

please return it to me."

I was ready to log off when Wax walked

over carrying an armload of books.

"Dribble, can you help me?" he asked.

"Here, take this book. I already checked it

out."

Wax gave me the book, and I carried it

past Mrs. Booker's desk.

"STOP this minute, Sam Dibble!" Mrs.

Booker shouted. "You should know better

than to sneak a reference book out of the

library!"

I looked at the book Wax had given me. It

had a bright-red sticker on the spine that said

Reference Only!

"Mrs. Booker, it's Max's book!" I tried to

explain. "He gave it to me."

Wax pointed to the title. "The book's

about Abraham Lincoln," he said. "That's the

president Sam picked."

HOW
I DID IT

REFERENCE ONLY

ABE LINCOLN

Mrs. Booker took the book from me and put it on her desk. "Did you give Sam this book?" she asked Wax.

Wax looked down at his feet. "Well, I guess I did. But he took it!"

"Don't let this happen again," Mrs. Booker scolded Wax.

HA-HA!

Then she turned to me and said, "Next time, look at the book before you take it out of the library."

"Dribble, no one's going to vote for a reference-book robber," Wax said as we walked home from school.

I didn't worry about what Wax said.

Everyone knew I didn't really steal the book.

Right?

Chapter Five
A Toilet Bowl Doodle

The next day, I promised my class that if they voted for me, we'd have quilted toilet paper in the bathroom.

"Nice try, Dribble," Wax said. "But I just took an exit poll of kids coming out of the bathroom, and they all said they're voting for me."

Now I've got to think of something else,

and it better be good!

The best part of the day

was when we had art. Miss

Murphy is the art teacher.

She's really nice, and she likes to doodle,

just like me. And she hangs up everyone's work

on the walls of her room. Some of them are my

doodles!

One day my doodles are going to be in an

art museum, but first I have to pass third grade.

"Welcome," Miss Murphy said. "Pull up a seat so we can get started." **start**

Rachel raised her hand. "Max, Sam, and I are running for class president," she explained. "Can we make campaign posters?"

"That's just what I had in mind for today," Miss Murphy said. "Posters use pictures and just a few words to teach something or change the way people think. Let's look at how they do that."

Everyone gathered around the art-room computer, and Miss Murphy showed us pictures of posters.

The one I liked the best was a poster of a

pro basketball player.

He was sitting at a table

reading a book, and it said

Get Smart—Read Books.

Grandpa Dibble told

me that when he was

a kid, they didn't have

books, so he had to read

the backs of cereal boxes.

"Poster board, markers, and paint are out

on the supply table," Miss Murphy told the

class.

"Max, Rachel, and Sam can work on their

campaign posters. Everyone else will design a

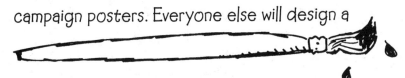

poster that encourages people to vote."

The tables in the art room were covered with brown paper. Miss Murphy said it's okay if we doodle on it. That's why I like her best.

I grabbed white poster board and markers and hurried to my table.

Rachel and Wax were already there, working on their posters.

"I'm writing a slogan—'Everyone Says: Rachel for Prez!'—on my poster," Rachel said. "And I'm going to draw a picture of myself."

Robert never told me I needed a slogan. I figured I'd better think of one quick.

I asked Miss Murphy for a hall pass to go

to the bathroom.

That's where I do

my best thinking.

When I walked into the bathroom, I had to

step over a puddle of water in the middle of

the floor.

Some kid had stuffed the sink with paper

towels and left the water running.

One time, Wax wrote my name on the

inside of the stall door. But no one thought I

did it because he spelled it wrong.

Sim Dobble,

I pulled down my pants and sat on the toilet seat. Then it came to me!

**THINK
↓HERE↓**

My campaign slogan was: "No Time to Poop, Get Off the Pot, Vote for Sam, Thanks a Lot!"

I hurried back to the art room. Rachel wasn't there, but she had left her poster facedown on the table.

"Hey, Dribble, check this out," Wax said, holding up his poster. "My slogan is: 'Roses Are Red, Candy Is Sweet, Vote for Me, or I'll Make You Smell My Feet!'"

When Rachel came back to our table, she

turned over her poster. "Oh no, it's ruined!"

she shouted. "Someone doodled on it!"

There was a blue mustache on it.

RACHEL
FOR PREZ!

Miss Murphy rushed over and asked what

happened.

"Dribble did it," Wax accused me. "He's

always doodling!"

"Sam, if this is true, I'll have to take away one of your stars for bad behavior," Miss Murphy said.

Miss Murphy gave a set of new colored pencils to the kid who got the most stars.

"It isn't my mustache," I tried to explain. "Mine would look lots better."

The bell was about to ring, and Miss Murphy told us to put away our art supplies. Wax stood up, and a marker fell out of his pocket!

And when he reached down to pick it up, there were fresh blue marker smudges on his hands!

Rachel pointed her finger at Wax. "Max Baxter, you're the meanest boy I know," she declared.

Miss Murphy told Wax that he was losing two stars. Then she helped Rachel paint over the mustache.

I want to beat Rachel in the election, but I was glad that she wasn't mad at me anymore!

Chapter Six
A Race Car Doodle

When we got back to class, I asked Mrs. H. where I could hang my poster.

She showed me a place, but said first I have to cross out the word *poop*.

I didn't think *poop* was such a bad word.

My cousin Arthur says it all the time, and he's only two years old.

"Take out your assignment notebooks," Mrs. H. said. "And copy your homework." This was my great idea: I'm telling everyone that if they vote for me, we won't get homework over the weekend. Here's why:

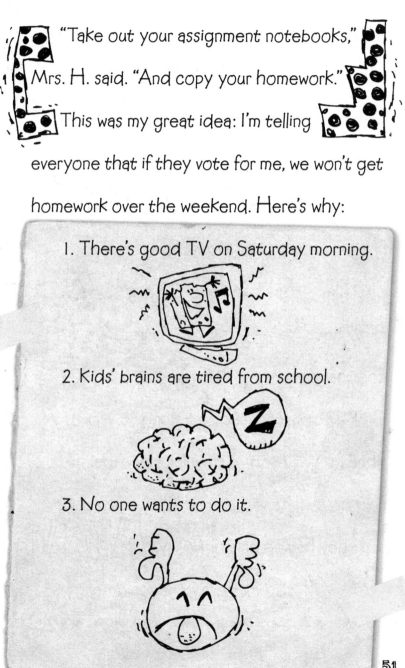

1. There's good TV on Saturday morning.

2. Kids' brains are tired from school.

3. No one wants to do it.

Before the last bell rang, Mrs. H. asked for someone to take Fluffernutter home a day early. Usually, someone takes her home over the weekend. But the classroom was being cleaned tonight, and Mrs. H. said the chemicals could be harmful to a hamster.

I guess they had to spray because Wax got cooties again.

Cootie →

Fluffernutter used to belong to Wax. But when he got tired of cleaning her cage, he told his dad he was allergic to hamster poop, and they had to give her away. HACHO

Mrs. H. said Fluffernutter could be our

class pet since no one was allergic except for

Wax, and he made that up.

My mom told Mrs. H. at the beginning

of school that I could take a pet home, so I

volunteered to take Fluffernutter.

Rachel fosters shelter dogs, and Wax

brags that he takes care of his little sister.

I wanted to show everyone that I could be

helpful, too.

"Thank you, Sam," Mrs. H. said when I

raised my hand. "Just remember the rules:

keep the water bottle filled, give her a cut-up

apple for a treat, and don't take Fluffernutter

out of her cage." **RULES**

That's because pets run away all the time.

One time my cat, Fang, ran away. When she

came back, she had a surprise.

 Fang is a long-haired rescue cat. She has

one blue eye and one green eye and teeth

that look like fangs.

 If I entered her in an ugly-cat contest,

she'd win first prize!

Robert's mom said he could come over

to my house and help me write my speech, so

Grandpa was picking us up after school.

When the last bell rang, we packed up our

things and headed to our lockers. **ONE WAY**

Wax was standing in front of his locker.

"Free limo rides!" he shouted. "Vote for Max

Baxter!" **Free**

"What's going on?" I asked Robert.

"Wax is giving free rides in his dad's limo to

anyone who votes for him."

Wax's dad owns a funeral home, and he touches dead bodies every day. When Mr. Baxter sees me, he wants to shake my hand. But I tell him I can't because I just picked my nose.

Grandpa's car was parked behind the limo in front of school.

Grandpa said he drove his car in the Indy 500, but he didn't win because he got a traffic ticket for going too fast.

While Wax was busy showing off his dad's limo, Robert and I hopped into the backseat of Grandpa's car.

I looked out the window and saw Mrs. H. She was carrying Fluffernutter's cage.

"Put it right here," Grandpa told her, pointing to the passenger seat.

Mrs. H. waved good-bye. "Have a good evening," she said. BYE

After Mrs. H. walked away, Grandpa revved the car's engine. "Fasten your seat belts, boys. The pedal's to the metal, and we're taking off!"

It's much more fun riding in Grandpa's car

than in a limo with a dead body!

Chapter Seven
A Pig Doodle

Grandpa left his car in the driveway because

my mom's car was parked in the garage.

I carried Fluffernutter's cage into the

kitchen. "Hello, Mom. We're home," I announced.

My mom was stirring a pot on the stove.

"Hi, boys," she said. Then she spotted

Fluffernutter's cage. "Sam, why do you have

the hamster?"

"Our classroom is being cleaned tonight,

and Mrs. H. didn't want Fluffernutter to die," I explained.

My mom gave me a strange look.

"She said the chemicals could be bad for

her," I said, pointing at the hamster. "Plus,

you told me I could take her home for the

weekend anytime, so I did. It's just a day early."

"But we're going away to visit your aunt and uncle this weekend. We can't take care of the hamster," my mom said.

Oops, I forgot about that.

"Well, we can keep her for the night at least," my mom said. "Just  put the cage in your room so she'll be safe."

The only thing that's safe in my room is the stash of candy I have hidden in my closet.

SHHHH...

Robert and I walked down the hall to

my bedroom. There was a sign taped to the

outside of my door.

Beware
ALL WHO enter!!!

1. No TOUCHING MY stuff
2. no LooKiNG under my bed
3. No eating my Halloween candy
4. No Farting, nose picking, or burping (except for me)

I peeked inside the cage. Fluffernutter was asleep in her hiding house.

Mrs. H. told us that some hamsters are nocturnal. That means they sleep during the day and are awake at night.

If I were nocturnal, I'd play video games all day and go to school at night.

When Robert and I walked back to the kitchen, my mom was busy frosting a fancy cake.

I reached into a box of chocolate chip cookies and passed one to Robert.

"Whaz gon on?" I mumbled with a mouth full of cookie.

"Don't you remember? We're having company for dinner—the Baxters."

I almost choked on my cookie. "WHAT?" I shouted. "Wax and Lucy are coming over here?"

My mom wiped her hands on a dish towel.
"I don't know where your head is lately. I told
you last night that they were coming. They
should be here any minute."

Here
it is!

I turned to Robert. "Call your mom and tell
her you want to stay for dinner," I pleaded.

The doorbell rang, and I took my time
getting it.

"Hello, young man," Wax's dad said, putting
out his hand to shake.

"Hello, Scribble Doodle," Lucy said, barging

into the hallway.

Lucy had pigtails that stuck out from the

sides of her head, and she was missing her two

front teeth.

Wax was close behind Lucy. "You should

quit the race for president, Dribble. My lead's

so big you'll never catch me."

My mom came into the hallway to greet

the Baxters, and I quickly pulled her aside.

"Why can't they eat in their own house?"

I whispered angrily.

"Sam, I'd like you and Max to be friends.
And Lucy looks up to you like an older
brother," my mom said.

"I don't want to be Lucy's big brother!"
I told her. "She's already got one!"

Grandpa stuck his head out of the dining
room. "Chow is on the table," he announced.

I sat down next to Robert at the dining-
room table. I wanted to get as far away from
Lucy as I could.

"I'm not eating," Lucy said. "I want to play in Sam's room."

"You can't!" I shouted. "I've got important stuff in there, like my bobbleheads and Halloween candy."

"Aw, why don't you let her?" Wax said. "She's not going to touch anything."

"Eat something first, Lucy dear," my mom suggested. "Then you can play in Sam's room."

Grandpa walked into the dining room
carrying a large covered pot. "It's 'roadkill
stew,'" he said, lifting off the lid. "Hope you
like it."

"Dad's only joking," my mom said, laughing.
"It's his delicious beef stew."

Lucy pinched her nose. "Ooh, it smells
bad! I'm going to play in Sam's room."

I watched as Lucy got up from the table
and ran down the hall.

"Don't worry about Lucy," Wax's dad said.
"I'm sure she'll find something to do in Sam's
room."

No way I wanted Lucy in my room!

I gulped down my dinner as fast as I could

and chased after her. I hoped I could stop her

before she did something disastrous!

Chapter Eight
A Wedgie Doodle

When I got to my room, I checked my

Halloween candy collection and bobbleheads.

Then I went straight over to Fluffernutter's

cage to see if she was okay.

Lucy was hopping up and down on one foot

in the middle of my room. "See what I can do,

Sam Nibble-Dibble," she said. "Bet you can't

do it."

"Lucy, where is the hamster?" I yelled. "Tell

me what you did with her!"

"You're mean," Lucy cried, sticking out her

tongue. "I'm telling Max you lost his hamster!"

"I didn't lose her, you did!" I shouted.

"Besides, she's not his anymore. Now tell me

where the hamster is!"

Lucy put her hands on her hips. "I'm not

telling," she said. "And you can't make me."

"Listen, Lucy, tell me where Fluffernutter is,

or I'm telling that you opened her cage and let

her out!"

"She ran away," Lucy said, whistling

between her missing front teeth.

Mrs. H. was counting on me to take care

of Fluffernutter.

"Keep your mouth shut," I threatened

Lucy. "If my class finds out what happened, no

one will vote for me."

73

Lucy hesitated a second. Then she said,

"I won't tell if you give me something, and it

better be good!"

I looked around my room. "How about

a bobblehead?" I offered. "It's a really

famous president."

Lucy shook her head. "Nope, I don't

want that. I want candy."

I dug in my closet and came up with a half-eaten candy bar left over from Halloween.

"Now don't say a word!" I warned Lucy, handing her the candy.

"Okay, Sammy Dribble-Bibble," she said. "I promise I won't tell anyone that you lost the hamster."

I hurried back to the dining room, and Lucy followed behind me.

"What took you so long?" Robert said when I sat down at the table.

"I'll tell you later," I whispered.

Grandpa tapped his water glass with his spoon. "I'd like your attention," he said. "Let's toast my grandson, Sam. He's about to be elected class president!"

If I don't find Fluffernutter, I'll be the class cleanup monitor and not the president!

"My Max wrote a great speech," Wax's dad said, ignoring what Grandpa had just said. "Did it all by himself, too."

HA!

"I helped Abe Lincoln write his Gettysburg Address," Grandpa said. "Turned out to be a big hit. Maybe you watched it on TV. It's in reruns now."

Yikes, I hadn't even written my speech, and we were supposed to give them tomorrow!

I asked to be excused from the table. Then I got ahold of Robert and dragged him back to my room.

"What's going on?" Robert asked. "It better be important since we're missing dessert."

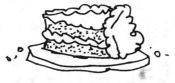

"Something really bad happened, and I'm in the worst trouble of my life!"

"Wow, is it worse than getting a wedgie with skid marks?" Robert asked.

I took a deep breath. "Lucy opened the cage, and Fluffernutter ran away!"

One time I ran away from home, but I was only gone for a few minutes because I didn't want to miss my favorite TV show.

Robert walked over to Fluffernutter's cage and looked inside.

"Yeah, she's missing, all right," he said, shaking his head. "But I can help you look for her."

HERE, FLUFFERNutter!

First, we looked under my bed, but all we

found was my dirty clothes and a moldy donut.

We were digging in my closet when

suddenly Wax barged into my room. "I came to

see my hamster," he said. "Where is she?"

"She's not yours anymore, Wax. You gave

her away, and now she's the class pet."

"Whatever, Dribble," Wax said, looking

around. "Where'd you put her?"

I quickly stood in front of the cage to block his view. "Hamsters sleep during the daytime, Wax. I don't want you to wake her up."

"Move aside, Dribble! I want to see her for myself."

When Wax bent down to look into Fluffernutter's cage, I grabbed hold of his underpants and tugged as hard as I could.

"WEDGIE!" I yelled. Then Robert and I took off running down the hall.

"I'll get you for this, Dribble," Wax shouted

as he chased after us.

The three of us burst into the dining room.

"It looks like you boys are having fun," my mom

said. "I'm so glad you're getting along."

Chapter Nine
A Math Test Doodle

I sat down at the table and saw Lucy. She

was sprawled out on the floor petting Fang.

"I want a pet," Lucy whined. "Daddy, buy

me one now!"

"Lucy, we've discussed this before. I'm not

getting you a pet. I don't have the time to

take care of one," Wax's dad said.

"Then how about you buy one for my

class? Max's class has a fish and a hamster, and

my class doesn't even have *one*!"

I looked over at Fang.

She was cleaning her paws

and licking her lips.

Suddenly, my heart started

racing, and it was hard to catch my

breath. It was the same way I feel

before I get my math tests back.

"Did you boys change your mind about

having dessert?" my mom asked, slicing into

the cake.

I couldn't eat a bite. What if Fang found

Fluffernutter and thought she was dessert?

After everyone finished eating, Mr. Baxter

said that it was time for them to go.

"We have to get home early so Max can

work on his acceptance speech," he told us.

"And I've got a busy day at the funeral home."

Maybe I'll come down

with hoof-and-mouth

disease, and I won't be

able to go back to

school tomorrow.

"Too bad you have to leave so soon,

Baxter," Grandpa said. "Let me show you to

the door."

Lucy grabbed my hand and shook it up and

down. "Bye-bye, Sam Doody-Dibble. You don't

have good toys, so I'm never coming back again."

"Max, don't forget your backpack," Wax's

dad said. "You left it by the door."

Wax came straight to my house from

after-school study hall. The only time I had to

go there was when I got detention.

"Good-bye, sweetheart," Wax's dad said.

Then he gave my mom a kiss. GROSS!

Wax tossed his backpack over his shoulder.

"Good luck with the election, Dribble," he said.

"You'll need it."

"Don't be so sure of that, Wax," I said,

shutting the door behind him.

After the Baxters left, my mom put her

arm around me. "Don't look so disappointed.

They'll come back soon."

TIGER
PIT
HA-
HA

Chapter Ten
A Twin Hamster Doodle

Robert and I walked back to my room. I sat down on my bed and stared at Fluffernutter's empty cage. **EMPTY WHY?**

"What are you going to do now?" Robert asked.

"I need to get my hands on some money!" I answered.

"Don't do it!" Robert said. "You can't run away. We still have to work on your speech."

"I'm not going anywhere. I need the money to buy a new hamster."

"Oh. What kind of hamster are you buying?"

"One that looks like Fluffernutter!"

My plan was to put the hamster into Fluffernutter's cage and fool everyone into thinking it was her.

I looked at the clock. It was just seven o'clock. There was still enough time for us to

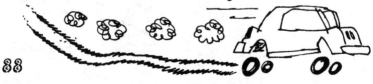

get to the pet store before it closed.

Robert and I found Grandpa in the living room. He was watching TV.

"Grandpa, can you take us to the pet store?" I asked. "I have to buy a hamster."

I told Grandpa what was going on. But I was afraid to tell my mom.

Instead, I just asked her if I could go to the pet store with Grandpa. She said I could go after I finished my homework.

But I made sure that Robert called his

mom to ask if he could go.

Robert's mom said it was okay as long as

he finished his homework. All moms

say the same thing. They must've

learned it in Mom School.

"Well then, let's go, Sammy-boy," Grandpa

said, putting on his coat.

The Tails & Scales Pet Store is not far

from my house. Cookie's older brother, Mike,

works there.

When we got inside the store, Mike was

waiting to greet us.

"Welcome to the city's largest selection of

pets," Mike said. "Is there something I can help

you find?"

Cookie told me Mike had to practice

saying that before they'd give him the job.

I looked around the store. It had birds,

fish, and small animals in glass cages.

"I need a hamster," I told Mike.

"What kind do you want?" Mike asked.

"We've got golden hamsters, dwarf hamsters,

short-haired hamsters, and long-haired

hamsters."

"Do you have one that's cute and has

peanut butter-colored fur?"

"Maybe. Follow me, and I'll show you what

we have."

Grandpa stayed behind to talk to the

parrot while Robert and I followed Mike to the

back of the store.

"Here they are," Mike said, pointing to a row of cages.

I looked inside all the cages. One hamster was black, and one was all brown. Another hamster was tan with a white spot on its nose, but I didn't see a hamster that looked just like Fluffernutter.

Then I spotted a hamster that kind of looked like Fluffernutter. It was light brown and cute, and I decided to buy it.

SOLD

"How much does this one cost?" I asked

Mike.

"That one's twenty bucks. Do you want

it?" **$ $ $!**

That was all my birthday and Christmas

money. I nodded my head, and Mike said he'd

put the hamster in a carrier box and bring it up

to the register.

I hoped my plan would work. If not, I'd be

out twenty bucks.

94

Chapter Eleven
A Candy Bar Doodle

I woke up early on Friday morning. This was

the biggest day of my life!

I put on my lucky

T-shirt. My cousin Ira gave

it to me. He won it at a

hot dog-eating contest.

After I got dressed, I walked into the

kitchen. My mom and Grandpa were eating

breakfast.

Grandpa looked up when he saw me.

"Howdy, Mr. President-to-be," he said. "Ready for your big day?"

My mom studied my face. "What's wrong, Sam? Aren't you feeling well?"

"I haven't even written my speech, and I don't even know what to say!"

"Just be true to yourself," my mom advised. "That's the best thing to do."

Then the doorbell rang. It had to be Cookie because I'd promised I'd give him a ride to school. I grabbed a toaster tart and ran to answer the door.

"Hi, Sam," Cookie said. "My brother, told

me you bought a new hamster. What'd you do

that for?"

"Promise you won't tell?"

Cookie crossed his heart and promised he

wouldn't tell, so I told him that Fluffernutter

was gone, and I had to get a new hamster that

looked like her.

"What if someone figures out it's not

Fluffernutter?" Cookie asked.

"Well, then I'll have to join the circus and

skip the rest of third grade."

"That would be so cool! Maybe I'll come with you," Cookie said, letting out a fart.

I brought the hamster's cage out to Grandpa's car and put it on the backseat between me and Cookie.

When we got to school, Wax was standing by the lockers handing out candy bars.

"Just a last-minute vote getter," Wax said. "Too bad you didn't think of it, Dribble."

"I don't need candy to get votes, Wax. But

you do!"

Then I quickly tried to sneak into the

classroom with Fluffernutter's cage, but Mrs.

H. spotted me.

"Why did you bring the hamster back?"

she asked.

"I forgot that we're going away for the

weekend, so I can't keep her," I said quickly.

Mrs. H. sighed. For a minute, I thought

she'd figured out that the hamster in the

cage wasn't Fluffernutter. Then she said, "Well,

I guess we can find someone else to take

her home over the weekend. But next time,

remember to clear things with your mother

first."

I didn't want to say anything else, so I just

nodded and raced to the back of the room. I

put the cage in the Science Corner.

I hoped that no one would get too

close and see that it wasn't Fluffernutter.

"Class, after I take attendance, we'll get

to the speeches," Mrs. H. said. "Rachel

will speak first, then Max, and then Sam."

I hurried to my desk. "Did you write your

speech?" Robert asked me.

"No, and I have to make up something, and

it has to be good!"

Mrs. H. finished taking attendance. "Okay,
Rachel. Let's hear your speech," she said.

Rachel walked up to the front of the room
and cleared her throat.

She said a lot of
things, but the only part
I heard was: "When I'm
president, we're going to
have more desserts for
lunch and a longer recess!"

Everyone applauded, and Rachel took a
bow. Next, Wax marched up to the front of
the room.

"I've got my speech right here," he said as

WAX'S SPEECH

he bent down and unzipped his backpack.

"A rat!" Meghan screamed. "It crawled out
of Wax's backpack!"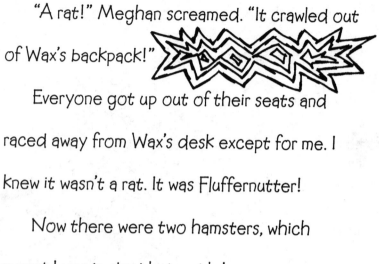
Everyone got up out of their seats and

raced away from Wax's desk except for me. I

knew it wasn't a rat. It was Fluffernutter!

Now there were two hamsters, which

meant I was in double trouble!

Chapter Twelve
A Fly Ball Doodle

I jumped up out of my seat and ran to

catch Fluffernutter.

"I won't let you get away this time," I

scolded as I scooped her up with my hand.

Wax just stood there

with his mouth wide open.

He looked like the time

he played outfield and

dropped a fly ball.

Rachel turned and faced Wax.  "I think you're trying to get Sam in trouble again," she said. "I bet you were the one who took Fluffernutter!"

"I didn't have anything to do with this," Wax said. "This is all Sam's fault!"

Mrs. H. told me to put Fluffernutter back in her cage.

Meghan walked over to the Science Corner with me. She wanted to make sure that Fluffernutter got there safely. Suddenly, she shouted, "Oh no! There's another hamster in Fluffernutter's cage!"

Mrs. H. stared at Wax with her laser eyes.

"Max Baxter, what do you know about this?"

"I didn't do anything . . . ," Wax said

tearfully. "And I don't know how Fluffernutter

got into my backpack."

Wax is the biggest baby. One time we

watched a scary movie, and he hid under his

coat the whole time.

Waaaa)

Next, Mrs. H. turned her laser eyes on me.

"Well, maybe Sam can explain what happened,"

she said.

PRISON

Sometimes no one believes you even when you tell the truth. Like the time I told Mrs. H. I couldn't do my homework because aliens kidnapped me, and she said I had to do it anyway.

"Well, Sam," Mrs. H. said, "we're waiting for your explanation."

I cleared my throat. "Fluffernutter escaped and hid in Wax's backpack. When I couldn't find her, I bought a new hamster and put it in her cage."

I could've told Mrs. H. the whole story—how Lucy opened the cage and let Fluffernutter escape and how I tried to fool everyone, but Lucy's just a little kid, and I didn't want to get her in trouble. Plus, now we have a new hamster!

"Thank you for telling the truth,"
Mrs. H. told me.

"I'm just like Honest Abe,"
I said with a smile.

Mrs. H. didn't smile. Instead,
she handed me a cardboard carrier.

"We'll keep Fluffernutter in here until we
find a home for the new hamster. And
Max, you can give your speech now."

Wax stood up and said, "I should be
president because I'm the most valuable player
on my Little League team, and if you vote for
me, I'll work harder than Dribble or Rachel!"

Then he bowed, and everyone clapped.

Next, it was my turn. I decided to do my

speech in rap: AHEM.

◻ "I'm Sam Dibble, and I'm running for prez.

◻ Listen up, here's what everyone says:

◁ Sam's really funny and very cool.

◢ He even likes to doodle in school.

◎ So vote for me, you won't be sad.

◎ When I'm president, you'll be glad!"

Everyone stood up and cheered. I looked

out at Robert, and he gave me two thumbs-up!

Mrs. H. told us that when a president takes the oath of office, he promises to defend the Constitution.

When I win the election, I'll promise to follow classroom rules, do my homework, and only doodle some of the time!

Chapter Thirteen
A Superhero Doodle

After the speeches, it was time to vote. Mrs. H. told everyone to write down their choice for president on a slip of paper, and she'd count the votes.

Cookie went up and down the aisles passing out the slips of paper. "Sam, your speech rocked," he said. "You're going to win!"

There were sixteen girls and ten boys in my class. If all the boys and four girls voted for me, then I would win the election.

Maybe math isn't so hard after all!

$$\int_{-\infty}^{\infty} e^{-x^2} dx = \sqrt{\pi} \div \textcircled{D}$$

$$\left(a_n \cos \frac{n\pi x}{L} + b_n \sin \frac{n\pi x}{L} \right)$$

$$x = \frac{-b \pm \sqrt{b^2 - 4ac}}{2a} \backslash W$$

"Mrs. Hennessey, what if it's a tie?"

Meghan asked.

"That's a good question, Meghan," Mrs.

H. said. "Then we would have a runoff vote,

and the class will choose between the two top

vote getters."

"Maybe the candidate who wins gets to pick the vice president," Robert suggested.

"That's a good idea," Mrs. H. said. "Okay, class, you can vote now."

I took out my pencil and wrote my name on the slip of paper. Then I turned it over and doodled on the back.

Billion Pounds

After a few minutes, Mrs. H. said, "Time's up! Cookie, please collect the ballots."

Cookie gathered the slips and put them on Mrs. H.'s desk. Then she went up to the board and put marks next to each name.

"Well, the first vote is for Max," Mrs. H. said, putting a mark next to his name.

Wax jumped up and down. "Yeah, I'm going to win!" he shouted.

SIT DOWN!

"Next, we have two votes for Rachel," Mrs. H. said, putting marks next to her name. "And another vote for Max."

Then there were four more votes for Rachel and none for me.

RACHEL ✓✓✓✓✓✓
WAX ✓✓
SAM

Then I got a vote. And another. And another!

Soon, Rachel and I were tied with six votes each.

6=6 easy math

Mrs. H. kept putting marks next to our names. It was going to be a close race.

I kept my fingers crossed that I'd win. I

wanted to cross my toes, but it was really hard with my shoes on.

OUCH!

After a few minutes, Mrs. H. said, "Well, it seems we have a clear winner. Rachel is our president. Sam came in second and Max third."

Wax said he wanted a recount because he lost the election.

FOWL!

All the girls gathered around Rachel. They hugged her and said she was great. Girls do silly things like that.

I felt kind of bad that I didn't win, but I was glad Wax wouldn't be president. And Rachel will be an all right class president, as long as she doesn't make me do girly things!

"Now Rachel will pick her vice president," Mrs. H. said.

It got so quiet in the room, I could hear the new hamster running on Fluffernutter's exercise wheel.

Rachel got up, and she thanked the class for their votes. "My vice president will be Sam Dibble," she said. "I picked him because he's funny and nice and a good doodler!"

Being vice president wasn't so bad, and

Mrs. H. says when Rachel's absent, I get to take her place. And maybe I'll make Wax be the cleanup monitor for a day!

Maybe next year I'll run for fourth-grade class president and win!

Two Months Later . . .

The president took a long time to answer our letters. Maybe he got busy walking his dog or answering other kids' letters.

He probably didn't have time to write to each of us, so instead he wrote the class one letter. In it, the president said we should get good grades and study hard. After Mrs. H.

finished reading the letter, she put it down on

her desk.

Oh, you know that new

hamster I bought?

Well, I gave it to Lucy's

kindergarten class.

She said she always wanted a pet, and if I

gave it to her class, she wouldn't call me names.

Right now, I'm working on a new doodle.

But that's another story.

About the Author

J. Press has taught millions of kids how to doodle. She majored in doodling at Syracuse University and went on to get a master of doodling at the University of Pittsburgh. At home she enjoys spending time doodling with her children and grandchildren. In her spare time she . . . guess what? You're right! She DOODLES

About the Illustrator

Michael Kline (Mikey) received a doctorate in applied graphite transference from Fizzywiggle Polytechnic and went on to deface (sorry, *illustrate*) over forty books for children, the most notable being one with J. Press involving an ambulance-chasing peanut. The deadly handsome artist calls Wichita, Kansas, home, where he lives with his very understanding wife, Vickie, felines Baxter and Felix, and two sons.